C000079428

POOR TROLL

POOR TROLL

The Story of
Ruebezahl and the Princess

Based on the story by J. K. A. Musäus

Retold and illustrated by
Fritz Eichenberg

Stemmer House
PUBLISHERS, INC.
OWINGS MILLS, MARYLAND

Text and illustrations © 1983 by Fritz Eichenberg
All rights reserved

No part of this book may be used or reproduced in any form or
in any manner whatsoever, electrical or mechanical, including
xerography, microfilm, recording and photocopying, without
written permission, except in the case of brief quotations in
critical articles and reviews.

Inquiries should be directed to
Stemmer House Publishers, Inc.
2627 Caves Road
Owings Mills, Maryland 21117

A Barbara Holdridge Book
Printed and bound in the United States of America
First Edition

Designed by Barbara Holdridge
Composed in Baskerville, with Art Gothic display,
by Service Composition Company, Baltimore, Maryland
Printed on 80-pound Mohawk Superfine paper by Federated
Lithographers-Printers, Inc., Providence, Rhode Island
Color separations by Capper, Inc., Knoxville, Tennessee
Jackets printed by Rugby, Inc., Knoxville, Tennessee
Bound in Holliston Lexitone Hunter Green, Kid Grain, and
Kivar Renaissance Saddle by Delmar Printing Company,
Charlotte, North Carolina

Library of Congress Cataloging in Publication Data

Eichenberg, Fritz, 1901-
   Poor troll.

   Adaptation of: Rübezahl / J. K. A. Musäus.
   Summary: The enchanted carrots Ruebezahl,
the mighty prince of the trolls, gives Princess
Emma provides her with a way to escape his
mountain palace.
   [1. Fairy tales.   2. Folklore—Germany.
3. Trolls—Fiction]   I. Musäus, Johann Karl
August, 1735-1787.   Rübezahl.   II. Title.
PZ8.E35Po   398.2'1'0943   82-795
ISBN 0-916144-94-1   AACR2

POOR TROLL

I<small>N THE VALLEYS</small> of the legendary Giant Mountains, in that part of Germany called Silesia, there lives the mighty spirit of the mountain, known as Ruebezahl, the "Carrot-Counter." The story of how he became known by such an odd name is told by the mountain folk of Silesia to this day.

This prince of the trolls, so the story goes, owns only a small part of the land's surface: a few square miles surrounded by a chain of mountains he shares with two neighboring rulers, who seem to ignore his existence.

But his sovereignty really begins just a short distance under the surface of the land. It reaches down 860 miles, straight to the center of this earth.

Every once in a while, it pleases this subterranean monarch to survey the endless treasure vaults, the cascades of precious gems and the layers of rare minerals of his vast underground empire, and to inspect the army of trolls who work for him.

But sometimes he tries to forget the cares of his hidden kingdom, decides to relax a bit in the vast mountains and to have some fun by playing jokes on the little humans, or by setting the wild animals to fight each other for his amusement.

When he grows bored with these games, he descends again into his subterranean regions to hide for a few centuries until he feels like relaxing in the sun again and enjoying the sights of the other world.

How astonished he was one day, looking down from the snow-covered crags, to discover a changed landscape. Where there had been dark forests before, he saw straw-covered roofs of prosperous villages among flowering orchards. Sheep and cattle were grazing in the meadows, and you could hear the sound of shepherds' flutes.

The novelty of this sight so pleased the astonished landlord that he felt like learning something more about these little human beings.

So one day he took on the appearance of a sturdy field hand and hired himself out to the first farmer he met on the way.

Unfortunately, his boss happened to be a wastrel who spent freely whatever his faithful servant had earned for him, and rarely rewarded him for his loyalty.

Disgusted, Ruebezahl went to work for a neighboring farmer, who gladly turned his flock over to him.

But this new boss was a pennypincher who paid him hardly anything for his good services.

Disappointed, Ruebezahl soon left the miser and started to serve the local judge.

But he soon found out that the judge bent the law for his own profit and made a mockery of justice.

In disgust, Ruebezahl withdrew to a mountain peak to ponder why Mother Nature would waste her gifts on such worthless people. Yet after a while, curiosity got the better of him. Once again he ventured out, invisibly, into the valleys below.

It happened one day, when he was hiding among the bushes and hedges, that he saw by chance the figure of a young girl, lovely as Venus, ready to slip into a pool. Her companions were lying around her in the grass at a waterfall which plunged into a natural basin, and they played and laughed in harmony with their mistress.

This image worked so powerfully on the watchful Lord of the Mountain that he almost forgot his other-worldly nature and longed to be a mortal. He changed himself into a black raven and flew to the top of a tall ash tree overlooking the pool, to enjoy this lovely spectacle. But quickly he discovered that now he saw everything with the eyes of a raven—and that a nest of field mice seemed more desirable to him than a bathing beauty.

Back he flew into the bushes and changed into a handsome youth, who felt emotions in his heart such as he had never experienced before. A powerful urge pulled him to the waterfall to get another glimpse of this beauty, the daughter of a king who ruled over that part of the mountains. She had often explored the forests with her companions to collect herbs and flowers, or to pick some wild cherries and strawberries for her father's table. On hot days it was her custom to take a dip in the pool at the waterfall.

From that moment on, the power of love drove the troll to this place day after day, where he waited impatiently for the return of the charming bathing party. And sure enough,

at the high noon of a sultry summer day, the princess and her escort again felt like visiting the cool shades at the waterfall.

You can easily imagine her astonishment when she found the place completely changed. The rough rocks were covered with marble and alabaster; the water did not plunge wildly down the mountainside but leapt softly step by step into a wide marble basin, from which a fountain rose and fell in a soft spray back into the pool. Wildflowers grew around the rim, and hedges of wild roses, mixed with jasmine and silverblossoms, formed a lovely natural stage. On both sides of the cascade opened two grottos whose walls were covered with sparkling crystals. Tasty refreshments were spread in various niches, inviting to be sampled.

The princess stood in silent wonder, hardly trusting her eyes. Should she enter this enchanted place—or make her escape?

However, she gave in to her irresistible desire to taste of the delicacies which seemed to await her. And, of course, after her explorations, she could not resist taking a little dip in the pool.

But no sooner had the lovely nymph slipped over the marble rim of the pool, than she quickly sank into a seemingly bottomless pit. Faster than her surprised companions could grasp her golden tresses, the treacherous water swallowed up their mistress.

The frightened girls cried for help as their lady disappeared before their eyes. They wrung their hands, prayed in vain for pity, and ran anxiously around the marble rim, while the fountain suddenly doused them with a heavy spray of water.

Yet no one dared to dive after their vanished mistress but Brunhild, her closest companion, who jumped quickly into the bottomless whirlpool, hoping to share the fate of her friend. Instead she found herself floating on the surface like a little cork, and try as hard as she could, she was not able to dive beneath the water.

There was nothing to be done but to tell the king of the sad fate of his daughter. Weeping and sobbing, they met him on his way to the hunt.

In grief and horror he tore his beard, covered his face with his purple cloak, and wept and moaned loudly over the loss of his lovely Emma. He hastened to the scene of the disaster, but the enchanted place had disappeared. Nature had taken on its former wildness—there was no grotto, no marble pool, no rose garden, no jasmine arbor.

POOR TROLL

The good king did not suspect that his daughter had been kidnapped by a knight-errant, since such things did not happen in his country in those days. He accepted the frightened maidens' story as truth, and concluded that Thor or Wotan or some other deity might have plotted this mysterious event. Continuing on his hunting trip, he soon accepted his sad loss.

In the meantime, our charming Emma didn't feel too wretched in the arms of her new suitor. After having whisked her away with his magic before the eyes of her young ladies, the Mountain King was now leading his lovely victim through an underground passage to a palace much more magnificent than her parental residence. With her spirits sufficiently revived, the little princess found herself on a comfortable sofa, in an elegant rose-colored satin dress with a blue sash. An attractive young man was lying at her feet, confessing his deepest love, which she blushingly accepted. The enchanted troll revealed to her his origin and rank, describing his subterranean empire. Leading her through the vast chambers and halls of his palace, he showed off all its splendid treasures.

Surrounding the palace was a beautiful park which, with its cool shades, seemed to please our lady most. The trees carried purple fruit sprinkled with gold. The bushes were alive with singing birds, an orchestra of many voices. But the lover had eyes only for his beloved, and his ear listened greedily to the sounds of her voice. In all of his immortal life he had never experienced such bliss.

Unhappily, our charming Emma did not feel the same ecstasy. Her soul was overshadowed by desires which she did not share with her new lover.

He discovered this soon enough, and tried through a thousand endearments to disperse those dark clouds and to amuse his beloved—in vain!

A human being, he told himself, is a social animal like the bee and the ant. These beautiful mortals, he realized, need entertainment. In whom could his lady-love confide? For whom might she dress up? How to flatter her? But after all—did he not have magic power?

Quickly he rushed to his fields, pulled out a dozen carrots, and arranged them in a pretty covered reed basket. He found beautiful Emma all alone in her shady green-house, plucking apart a little rose.

"Most beautiful of all mortal women," said the distressed troll, "you shall never be lonely any more! Everything you need to make life more pleasant is in this basket. With the

touch of this little magic wand you can turn these earthy roots into any being you desire!"

Our eager princess didn't lose any time in using the wand as directed. "Brunhild," she called, "dear Brunhild, appear!" And right away her favorite friend was lying at her feet, embracing the knees of her mistress, shedding tears of joy and holding her arms as she so often had done before.

The deception was so complete that even Emma couldn't tell if she had created the real Brunhild—or a mirage!

But she abandoned herself completely to the pleasures of being with her dearest companion, strolling with her hand in hand through the garden, letting her admire the dazzling landscape, and plucking gold-speckled apples from the trees. Then she guided Brunhild through all the rooms of the palace, especially investigating the wardrobe room, where they tried on all the veils and belts and jewels till the sun went down. In fact the so-called Brunhild showed so much taste in the selection of milady's dresses, that even if she was by nature only a carrot, no one could deny her the glory of being the finest of her species.

Beautiful Emma appeared to the lord of the mansion lovelier, friendlier and gayer than ever. She continued to transform his whole supply of carrots, turning them into her familiar ladies-in-waiting, and reserved the last two carrots to create her favorite cat and her little lapdog Beni.

When she had reassembled her whole little court, she assigned each of her ladies a special task, and never was a mistress served better! Her every wish was followed without question.

For several weeks Emma fully enjoyed her accustomed pleasures—dancing, songs and music in turn from morning till evening. But after a while the little princess noticed that the fresh skin of her playmates seemed to fade. She saw in the marble-hall mirror that she alone looked like a fresh rosebud, and that her beloved Brunhild and the other maidens began to resemble wilted flowers. Yet they all assured her that they felt fine, and the generous host indeed did everything to feed them well at his table. Nevertheless the ladies continued to shrink visibly, and life and vitality diminished from day to day.

One fine morning when the princess, refreshed by sound sleep, entered the ballroom, she was shocked to see a crowd of withered matrons staggering towards her on canes and crutches, coughing and wheezing pitifully, unable to straighten their backs. Even playful Beni was stretched on his back, and the cat could hardly move her legs.

24

POOR TROLL

In great distress the princess rushed out of the room to escape this gruesome company. She stepped out on the balcony and shouted for the troll, who quickly appeared, looking guilty.

"Malicious spirit," she cried out furiously, "why do you begrudge me the only joy of my sad life, the ghostly company of my former playmates? Is this solitude not punishment enough? Do you want to change this place into a graveyard? Return my companions to youth and beauty this very minute—or I will punish you for your misdeeds with my hatred and revulsion!"

"Most beautiful of all mortal maidens," replied the unhappy troll, "don't go too far in your anger. Everything in my power is at your command, but don't ask me for the impossible. The forces of nature obey me, but I can't change their immutable laws. As long as those carrots were full of their vital juices, the magic wand could change their vegetable lives according to your wishes. Now that their sap is used up, they shrink and decay. But, my beloved, let that not disburb you. A freshly filled basket will soon make up for the damage, and you can call your favorites to life again as you desire."

At this the distressed troll took his leave. Angry Emma touched the ladies with her magic wand, turned them into dried-up carrots and did what children do when they get tired of their toys: she threw them in the garbage heap and eagerly she skipped along the green lawn to pick up a freshly filled basket. She looked everywhere but couldn't find it. Soon she saw the troll approaching her, evidently greatly embarrassed.

"You have deceived me again," cried Emma. "Where is the basket?"

"Sweet ruler of my heart," begged the sheepish troll, "forgive my carelessness—I promised more than I could keep. I searched the whole countryside for carrots, but they were harvested last season and are rotting in dark cellars. Winter came to the valley, the fields look sad. It was your presence only that brought spring to these hills and flowers blossoming under your feet. I beg you—have patience for three months and you will again have a great time with your companions!"

The eloquent troll had barely finished his speech when lovely Emma turned her back on him and went to her room in a huff. The unhappy troll, disguised as a farmer, hurried to the nearest market place in his territory, and bought a

donkey which he loaded with heavy sacks of carrot seeds. He sowed them over a whole acre, and ordered his servants to start an underground fire to hasten the growth of his crop with gentle heat, like pineapples in a hothouse.

The carrots soon began to sprout, and promised a rich harvest in a short time. Every day Miss Emma went out to watch the crop, which meant more to her than all the golden apples. Yet dark thoughts and despair clouded her cornflower eyes. She hid in the dark shades of the pine woods, near a little brook which spilled its silver waters into the valley.

But the troll, being a novice in his studies of human nature, could not guess the real reason for his sweet mistress's bad moods.

He did not know that Prince Ratibor, a young neighbor, had captured the princess's heart. It was her first love, which, they say, is more invincible than any force of nature. Shortly before Emma's abduction, the young couple had decided to get married. The dreadful news of her disappearance had changed the love-stricken Ratibor into a maniac. He had left his castle, sought refuge in the lonely forests, and confided his despair to the silent mountains. Meanwhile, faithful Emma—hiding her secret grief—had tried for some time to find a way to outwit her captor and escape her lovely prison. After many sleepless nights, she had finally devised a plan which seemed to have a fair chance of succeeding.

Spring had returned to the mountain valley. The troll banked the fires under his crop, and the carrots, not touched by the winter's cold, began to ripen. Every day, Emma pulled out a few to experiment with, giving them various forms, apparently for her amusement.

But her real intentions went much further. One bright day she changed a little carrot into a bee.

"Fly towards the sun, little bee," she said. "Find Prince Ratibor, buzz softly into his ear that his Emma still lives for him, but that she is the slave of the Prince of the Trolls who lives under the mountains. Remember every word, and bring back Ratibor's message to me."

The bee took off from her mistress's finger, but a greedy swallow pounced on her and buried the ambassador of love in her crop.

Distressed but undaunted, Emma took another carrot and changed it into a cricket to teach her the same message. "Jump, little cricket, over the mountains to Prince Ratibor, and chirp into his ear that faithful Emma wishes to be freed from her bondage by his strong arms."

The cricket hopped as fast as she could to follow her orders. But a long-legged stork crossed her path, grabbed her with his beak and swallowed her.

Emma was not easily discouraged. To the third carrot she gave the shape of a magpie. "Fly away, you talkative bird," she said, "from tree to tree, until you reach my beloved Ratibor. Tell him about my imprisonment, and ask him to wait for me with his horse and men three days from now, at the border of May Valley, ready to rescue me and take me into his arms!"

The magpie obeyed. She flew from one resting place to the next, and Emma followed her flight anxiously, as far as the eye could see.

The heartbroken Ratibor was still roaming the forests. He sat under a shady oak, thought of his princess and deeply sighed: "Emma!" The echo softly carried back her beloved name, but an unfamiliar voice repeated it. Startled, he looked around. Not seeing anyone, he thought he was imagining things.

But then he heard his own name. He saw a magpie hopping from branch to branch and realized that the bird was calling him.

"Foolish gossip," he said, "who taught you the name of

an unfortunate who is eager to leave this world in order to forget his grief?" Angrily he grabbed a rock to throw it at the bird, when it pronounced the name "Emma" again. That stopped his hand, trembling with excitement, while her dear name echoed in his heart. With a magpie's inborn talent, the bird in the tree began to repeat the message it had been taught. Prince Ratibor was filled with delight. The deep sorrow that had clouded his mind vanished, reason and joy in living returned, and he eagerly asked the bird for more news about Emma's adventures. But the talkative magpie could only repeat its message over and over again, and flew away.

Lightheartedly, the revived Prince rushed back to his castle, quickly gathered a troop of his horsemen and departed with them, ready to do battle.

In the meantime, clever Emma prepared everything according to her plans. She stopped torturing the patient troll with her coldness. Her eyes promised hope, her stubborn resistance seemed to melt. Such happy signs were not lost on her love-struck suitor. He became bolder, renewed his courting, begged for her favor and this time, seemingly, was not rejected. The wedding was a foregone conclusion, on the condition that she might take another

day to think things over. The happy troll readily consented.

The following morning, shortly after sunrise, beautiful Emma appeared dressed like a bride, covered with jewels from her treasure chest. Her golden hair was adorned with a myrtle wreath, her dress glistened with gems, and she shyly covered her blushing face with a veil.

"Heavenly maiden!" stammered the troll. "Don't deprive me any longer of the promising glance which will make me the happiest creature the sun has ever seen!"

But the bride-to-be only wrapped herself more tightly in her veil and coyly said: "How can any mortal resist you, ruler of my heart? Your persistence has won me over. Take the promise from my lips but let the veil hide my blushes and my tears! My heart responds to your tenderness, but dark forebodings disturb my soul. *You* never age, but my mortal beauty is like a flower that soon will wilt. How can I be sure that you will always be tender and generous as a husband as you have been as my lover?"

"Ask me for any proof of my faithfulness or obedience in following your commands," he answered. "And judge from that the power of my eternal love!"

"So be it!" quickly replied clever Emma. "I want only one proof of your sincerity. Go and count all the carrots in your field. I cannot have a wedding without witnesses. I will create them to serve as my bridesmaids. But be careful not to deceive me, and take an accurate count, as this is the final test of your faithfulness.''

Although he hesitated to leave his charming bride alone even for one minute, the troll rushed off to count his carrots, and at first he thought he did quite well. But to be absolutely sure he repeated the count and found, to his dismay, a mistake which made it necessary to go over his rows a third time. Yet again he arrived at a different figure. No wonder—on such an important day any brain can get confused!

No sooner had the clever Emma seen her suitor disappear than she prepared for her own escape. For that purpose she had kept in readiness an especially juicy, well-developed carrot, which she quickly changed into a lively charger, complete with rein and saddle. She jumped on his back and raced across heath and meadows as fast as she could. The fine horse carried her swiftly, without stumbling, down into May Valley where, at the appointed spot, she happily threw herself into the arms of her anxiously waiting Ratibor.

The busy troll in the meantime had become so involved in the counting of his carrots that he was hardly aware of what went on around him.

After concentrating all his mental powers on his task, he finally succeeded in determining the exact figure of all the carrots in his field, big and small. Happily he rushed back to present his account to the ruler of his heart, to prove that he would certainly make the most obedient husband.

Highly pleased with himself, he ran through all the paths and arbors of his park without finding what he was looking for. He rushed to his palace, searched every nook and corner, calling the sweet name of Emma, but there was no response. Only the echo of her name rang through the empty halls. Now the troll became suspicious; he sensed foul play. Quickly he shed his human form, swung himself high into the air; just in time to see, in the distance, his beloved crossing the border on her swift charger.

Furiously the troll seized a heavy thunderbolt out of some peaceful clouds just passing by and threw it after the fugitive, making matchsticks out of a thousand-year-old oak that had guarded the border. Beyond it the troll's power did not reach, and the clouds dissolved in a gentle smoke. In despair, the disappointed lover returned to his palace, shuffling through the empty rooms and filling them with sighs and moans. Once again he visited the park, which held no more enchantment for him. He remembered every spot where Emma had walked, where she had picked flowers, where they had held most intimate conversations. It choked him up so much that he sank into deep melancholy. But soon this gave way to a raging fury, and he vowed to turn his back on the human race, never again to pay the least attention to this treacherous species.

In a mad rage he stamped the earth three times, and the wilderness took over again. A gaping abyss opened and the troll rushed down it to the deepest recess of his territory —the center of the Earth.

Even while the mountains were in upheaval, happy Prince Ratibor hurried his beautiful bounty to a safe place. He returned Emma to her father's court, where a splendid marriage took place. Afterwards the prince shared with her the throne of his realm, and built the city of Ratibor which carries his name to this day.

These strange adventures of Princess Emma in the Giant Mountains—her capture, her bold escape, her final rescue —became the legend of the land, passed on from generation to generation, even to our own day.

The inhabitants of the surrounding countryside never knew the real name of their formidable neighbor, who seemed to reappear in different disguises throughout the

centuries. Some feared him, some liked him well, according to their experiences. But after the princess escaped, everyone called him Ruebezahl, "Carrot Counter," in our language. To the great disgust of the mighty spirit, the name stuck, reminding him ever after of his most unlucky love affair.

And to this day, in the Giant Mountains of Silesia, it seems unwise to shout, or even whisper, the name "Ruebezahl." What kind of trouble it may cause no one knows, because no one—man, woman or child—has ever dared to taunt poor "Carrot Counter" and take a chance!